I0451864

Diary of a Not Normal Child

PRAISE FOR *STORYSHARES*

"One of the brightest innovators and game-changers in the education industry."
– Forbes

"Your success in applying research-validated practices to promote literacy serves as a valuable model for other organizations seeking to create evidence-based literacy programs."

- Library of Congress

"We need powerful social and educational innovation, and Storyshares is breaking new ground. The organization addresses critical problems facing our students and teachers. I am excited about the strategies it brings to the collective work of making sure every student has an equal chance in life."
– Teach For America

"Around the world, this is one of the up-and-coming trailblazers changing the landscape of literacy and education."
- International Literacy Association

"It's the perfect idea. There's really nothing like this. I mean wow, this will be a wonderful experience for young people."   - Andrea Davis Pinkney, Executive Director, Scholastic

"Reading for meaning opens opportunities for a lifetime of learning. Providing emerging readers with engaging texts that are designed to offer both challenges and support for each individual will improve their lives for years to come. Storyshares is a wonderful start."
- David Rose, Co-founder of CAST & UDL

Diary of a Not Normal Child

YuBin Park

STORYSHARES

Story Share, Inc.
New York. Boston. Philadelphia.

Diary of a Not Normal Child

Copyright © 2022 by Yubin Park

All rights reserved.

Published in the United States by Story Share, Inc.

The characters and events in this book are fictitious. Any similarity to real persons, living or dead, is entirely coincidental.

Storyshares
Story Share, Inc.
24 N. Bryn Mawr Avenue #340
Bryn Mawr, PA 19010-3304
www.storyshares.org

Inspiring reading with a new kind of book.

Interest Level: Middle School
Grade Level Equivalent: 3.3

9798885979429

Book design by Storyshares

Printed in the United States of America

Storyshares Presents

1

"Wake up, Itanya!" I woke to my mother's voice. "It's time to go to work!"

"Okay," I answer.

My name is Itanya and I work in a factory next to the house I share with my mom and little sister Mhina. She is 8 years old, and instead of coming to the factory with us, it is her responsibility to get water from a well in a neighboring village. I'm 12. There's not really anything especially interesting about our family, or me. Except that

I have a bird tattoo on my ankle. Mom says that Dad drew it there when I was 3, a year before he went to heaven.

"Mom, why are we so poor?" I asked, walking side-by-side with her to the factory. It was no secret that we only had just enough to get food.

"I told you not to ask that," she said. Her face looked serious, and we were quiet the rest of the way to work.

When we arrived, we each got into our positions and began working.

The whole day, I couldn't push my curiosity away. *Why wouldn't she tell me why we were so poor?*

I thought about it all day while I was working. Maybe my dad lost all his money when he died. Maybe we had just been poor when I was born in the first place.

Back home that night, I heard my mom saying to herself, "should we go back to the western part? What should I do?"

That made no sense to me. *What was the western part? The western part of Kenya?*

2

After another day in the factory, we came home to Mhina preparing dinner. When someone thinks of dinner, they probably think of a feast and wonderful food. But, to our family, it isn't. Our dinner is usually one bread with one cup of water. Mom, Mhina and I always eat all our food.

Afterwards was bed, and while I waited to fall asleep, I thought of how I want to live a normal life like other children. Other children can eat until they are full. Actually, I don't know what full means. I know the definition, but I don't know what is feels like. I can't even imagine it. And you know what's weird? I once heard that some children are forced to eat, even when they don't want to. I can't imagine that either.

These days, we are starving more than usual because the factory is not doing well.

Another thing about being a normal child would be that I could go to school. There is no school in our village. It is a sad thing to not be able to learn. I heard that the children who live normally sometimes hate to go to school. *Why?* Learning is a good thing. If I could get educated, I would love to go to school. *How can they hate school?* Maybe normal kids don't know about kids like us. Maybe they dont know how sad it is to not be educated.

3

On Sundays, I didn't need to go to work. Which was good, but also bad, since I couldn't earn money on those days. Mom went to another factory to earn money. I took care of my sister.

We started our Sundays at 5 o' clock in the morning. The first thing we needed do was get water from a well, which was about a few kilometers away from our house.

One particular Sunday, I called Mhina. "Mhina, come! Let's go get some water!"

"I'm coming!" she called back to me. Mom had already gone to the factory. Mhina and I held hands and went to get water. The land was light brown and there was only one tree. We walked along the path with a water bucket and a canteen for my sister.

The sun was rising. It was beautiful. And I could see wonderful birds soaring above my head. A bird is a symbol for hope. The sunrise means hope too. I paused, looking at the beautiful sunrise and wonderful birds.

One of the birds looked familiar. After I had thought for a second, I realized that it was the same bird as the one on my tattoo. Maybe I already had my own hope.

4

One day after work at the factory, my mom looked really ill.

"Mom, are you okay?" I asked.

"I'm just tired," she replied. I didn't know what else to say. We walked towards home.

When we arrived, we looked for Mhina. Usually, Mhina always went to get water 2 hours before we came home. It was weird that Mhina wasn't home. Maybe she had an accident. I was very worried. I went to go out and find her but my mom stopped me.

"Mhina will come back," she said. "Maybe she went out late."

The sun was low when Mhina came back. She looked very tired and she was limping. I called my mom. She came running towards Mhina.

"What happened Mhina?" she asked.

"I just fell down."

My mom looked really worried.

"Well then, I'll prepare dinner. You go to rest," I said.

That day was a bad feeling day. A no hope day. Mhina had got hurt, so we had little water. Mom looked sick. I had a feeling that there would be even worse thing happening.

After work the next day, I went to get water with my bucket. There was no sunrise and no birds soaring this time. It took a long time to get the water. My hope dwindled.

5

When I came back home, Mhina was crying. "Mom fainted!" she yelled. "Help Itanya, I cant do anything!"

I ran to mom and tried to check for a fever. Her head was as hot as a fireball. I didn't know what to do. I could only pray for her.

I tried to behave like an adult for Minha. But tears rolled down my face.

6

When I woke up the next day, I wished for it to be better than the day before, but nothing had really changed. Mhina still needed to rest. Mom was only just able to stand up, but she insisted on working, which made her sicker by the hour. I tried to stop her and send her home but said no. She worked all day long. Her condition got worse. By the end of the day, she couldn't even hold a canteen. Mhina had gotten worse too. She could no longer walk.

I couldn't remember what hope felt like. Maybe the birds and the sunset had meant nothing at all. I cried and I prayed.

7

Soon, mom could hardly breathe. None of the villagers helped us. I don't know if they couldn't or wouldn't. I screamed aloud. I thought I was going crazy. I thought I'd rather be dead.

8

A few days later, Mhina exclaimed, "Itanya! A NGO is coming this way!"

At first I couldn't speak. "We are saved!" I finally cried. "An NGO!"

Even though I hadn't gotten any education, I had learned some words from my dad before he went to heaven. I knew that NGOs could save us and give us food.

Mom had tears forming in her eyes. She was going to be saved and so was my sister! It was wonderful. All the villagers were coming out to the street and dancing. I carried Minha out and we danced too.

When the NGOs came, all the villagers welcomed them including us. "We are saved!"

We all started running towards the vehicles when a white person said, "we are giving out food!" I lined up with the others and waited for my turn. I wrote down my name, age, and home address and took a pot of food.

The next day, I didn't have to go to the factory. Instead, the NGO team invited all the villagers to a community meal to give us time to rest and eat while they listened to us and our needs. When it was my turn to talk, I talked about my mom and my sister.

9

The NGOs treated Minha's leg and with food and rest, mom was getting better. I found out what it felt like to be full.

The day the NGO's were leaving, there was an especially bright sunrise. Birds were everywhere.

One person from the NGO group came over to me and sat me down. She said that a girl my age from far away wanted to send me thirty dollars every month! That girl also wanted to send me letters, and maybe someday, visit me, if she could.

I cried with joy. It was a very, very good thing. We would have food. We would have water. Mom wouldn't have to work so much. Me and Minha could even go to school.

10

Since that day, I've had a dream I never would have dared to dream.

I dream that I will someday become a teacher who teaches children that are not educated because of their family's economic problems. I will be a teacher who cares for everyone and is fair to everyone no matter how much money they have. I will always help my students even if their behavior is bad. I will be a wonderful teacher. I will always try to learn everything that I can so that I can share my experience and knowledge with my students and better understand their different circumstances.

Most of all, I will give hope to my students. I know how important hope can be.

About The Author

Yubin Park is a 5th grader at The Branksome Hall School. Her hobbies include reading books, matching puzzles, and making arts and crafts. This year, she started participating in the Good Neighbors program, a humanitarian effort committed to educating children and developing communities in 35 countries around the world. She has been paired with a Kenyan girl, Anne Wakonyo, who is the inspiration for the main character of this story, Itanya. Yubin hopes to continue to support and learn alongside Anne.

About The Publisher

Story Shares is a nonprofit focused on supporting the millions of teens and adults who struggle with reading by creating a new shelf in the library specifically for them. The ever-growing collection features content that is compelling and culturally relevant for teens and adults, yet still readable at a range of lower reading levels.

Story Shares generates content by engaging deeply with writers, bringing together a community to create this new kind of book. With more intriguing and approachable stories to choose from, the teens and adults who have fallen behind are improving their skills and beginning to discover the joy of reading. For more information, visit storyshares.org.

Easy to Read. Hard to Put Down.

www.ingramcontent.com/pod-product-compliance
Lightning Source LLC
Chambersburg PA
CBHW071230170626
46809CB00005BA/2013

* 9 7 9 8 8 8 5 9 7 9 4 2 9 *